A pale purple lilac, a yellow rose, a blue hydrangea and a red rose,
For always and forever — my dear P.

Natacha

For Elisa.

Giorgio

General Manager: Gauthier Auzou
Senior Editor: Maya Saenz
English Version Editor: Rebecca Frazer
Translation from French: Susan Allen-Maurin
Layout: Annaïs Tassone
Production: Amélie Moncarré

Original Title: *La Reine des Neiges*
© Auzou Publishing, Paris (France), 2013 (English version)
ISBN: 978-2-7338-2530-3

Printed and bound in China, June 2013.

The Snow Queen

Adapted from the fairytale by Hans Christian Andersen
Text by Natacha Godeau
Illustrations by Giorgio Baroni

This is the story of Kay and Gerda—two friends as close as brother and sister. And it was their friendship that caused the nastiest of trolls to create the most horrifying invention.

"I detest nothing more than grace and kindness!" the old troll declared. He was busily working on his evil creation—a magic mirror that reflected the most beautiful things in the most horrible ways: a smile would become a frown, the colors of a beautiful landscape would fade, and beauty marks would turn into warts and disfigure a lovely face.

The troll was incredibly proud of his ingenious work. In fact, he decided to try his magic mirror on the most beautiful creatures of all... Heaven's angels! So he lifted his prized possession high above the clouds so it would reflect the wonders of Paradise. But, the weight of the mirror caused his arms to fiercely shake until it slipped from the troll's grasp and crashed to Earth, shattering into thousands of sharp pieces. Some of the glass splinters were so tiny that they floated with the wind, waiting to be blown into the eye of an innocent person.

Meanwhile, back on Earth, Kay and Gerda delighted in warm summer days. Their parents planted beautiful flowers in the window boxes that ran between their neighboring houses. The children would climb over the boxes and sit high above their tiny, rose-bordered garden.

But when winter arrived, their beloved garden was covered in snow. So, the children would heat a copper coin and place it on the ice-covered windowpane. It melted the ice away and they were able to see their garden through the little peep-hole.

It was during a cold, winter night that a sharp sting caused Kay to cry out.

"I've got something in my eye!" he said. "And there's a pain in my heart!"
But the pain eased and Kay soon felt better.

However, two splinters from the magic mirror had just penetrated his body.
Slowly but surely, they would deform his vision and turn his heart to ice.

The next night, Kay went sledding without Gerda. It was the perfect night and big, fat snowflakes were piling up. Kay wanted to go faster and faster, so when he found a sled in the moonlit square, he tied it to his and immediately accelerated down the hill.

He was whizzing down a small street when a feeling of horror came over him. A woman in a white hooded cloak approached him... it was the Snow Queen!

"Are you cold?" she asked, kissing his forehead.

And with that kiss, Kay's hair turned silver and his whole body turned to ice. The memories of his past life simply disappeared. In an instant, he was flying fearlessly away with the Snow Queen in the bitterly cold wind.

And Kay was never to be seen again.

It was a long, sad winter for Gerda. Until one morning, the following spring, she heard the swallows tweeting, "Let's sing! The sun is here to dry our tears!"

Gerda agreed. But, she remained convinced that Kay was lost, so she decided to search for him.

She ran down to the river where she climbed into a small boat to get a better view into the distance. But the boat drifted from the shore.

Gerda sailed and sailed until an old woman beckoned her back to dry land.

"I'm looking for my friend, Kay," Gerda replied.

"Come and wait for him inside," suggested the woman.

Gerda accepted the woman's offer. But, little did she know, the woman was actually a selfish sorceress who only wanted the child's company. She cast a spell on Gerda, causing the young girl to lose her memory. And then she cast another spell that caused all the rose bushes to sink into the earth so their scent wouldn't remind the girl of her own garden. And it worked... until the morning Gerda noticed a small, embroidered rose on the woman's hat.

She searched and searched for some real roses. And when she didn't find any, she wept. Her tears watered the ground and the rose bushes sprung up through the earth. Gerda's memory then flooded back to her!

And so Gerda decided to leave the old woman and continue searching for her friend. She traveled far and wide. One day, a big raven landed near her. "What are you doing all alone in the big, wide world?" it cawed.

"I've lost my friend," Gerda replied. "Have you seen him?"

The raven nodded. "I think so," he replied. "I know of a brave young boy who walked through the palace gates."

"It must be Kay!" exclaimed Gerda.

"He married the princess," the raven told her. "Now he is a prince! I will take you to him."

The bird and the girl set out to find Kay. They searched the palace until they found the grand royal bedroom. Gerda was astonished to see that the prince and princess were fast asleep. She softly approached the prince's bed and peered at him.

"It isn't Kay!" she gasped.

The princess awoke and was startled to find Gerda standing before her. Gerda quickly explained her search for her lost friend. The princess kindly gave her a velvet muff, a pair of boots, and a golden horse-drawn carriage. After a warm farewell, Gerda drove away in the beautiful stagecoach.

But, Gerda's travel had only begun when a band of robbers threatened her with a knife. Luckily, the band leader's daughter cried in protest.

"I want her to be my friend!" she shouted. And then, she jumped into the carriage with Gerda and they jolted away. When Gerda explained that she was looking for Kay, the young robber smiled.

"You must really love him!" she teased.

"Let's go. You're coming with me to our den."

And soon, they stopped in front of an old, rundown manor. Gerda noticed some soup boiling in a cauldron over a fire, a pair of pigeons in a cage, and a reindeer tethered to a post.

"Now tell me about Kay," the girl ordered. Gerda obeyed and told her all about her friend.

"We have seen him," the pigeons cooed. "He was on the Snow Queen's sled and they were on their way to Finland."

"My country," sighed the reindeer, nostalgically.

"I will help you," the girl said. "In exchange for your velvet muff."

"You must take Gerda to find her friend!" the young robber told the reindeer as she untied it from the post.

The reindeer leapt with joy. Gerda climbed onto the animal's back and they galloped away, into the cold North wind and over the frozen plains.

When they reached Finland, they knocked on the small door of a low house with a roof that touched the ground. A woman appeared and the reindeer politely asked her the way.

"The Snow Queen lives in the North where pink and green lights illuminate the sky," she told them.

They continued their journey
until they met another woman who
happened to be a magician. "Do you have
a potion to help Gerda rescue Kay?" asked the
reindeer. The magician shook her head.
"Gerda has all the power she needs," the woman replied.
"She will save the boy by removing the harmful splinters
from his body. Take her to the Snow Queen's garden.
She has gone South so the girl should enter easily."
Gerda headed to the Snow Queen's garden with fear in
her heart. But she forged on through the icy and bitter
cold snow bursts until she entered the palace.

And there was Kay!
He was standing in the middle of the cracked surface of a frozen lake,
blue and shivering from the cold.

"Dear Kay!" Gerda exclaimed and she jumped into her friend's arms.
But Kay's memories had been erased. He had forgotten her.

Gerda wept and wept. Her friend was gone. As she cried, warm tears washed over Kay and his frozen heart began to thaw. Kay then shed a single tear. And within that tear were the two tiny pieces of glass that had erased his memory and turned his heart to ice.

"My dear Gerda!" he exclaimed as his memory returned.

The two friends hugged each other tightly.
And they danced for joy, as they were free at last.

"Hooray!" shouted Kay. His cheeks turned rosy and
his hair became brown once again. Then, hand in hand,
the children left the frosty palace.

The next day, they began their journey home. It was spring by the time they reached the edge of their town. As they climbed the final steps of their journey, they realized they must have been gone for several years. They had grown so much, yet they were still children at heart.

Immediately, they looked at their beloved garden. The roses were still there, blooming in the sun. Gerda and Kay sat between the window boxes as they did so many years ago.

And as Kay sat thinking, he realized that the greatest gifts in life were those Gerda had given him—friendship and love.